THE ARABIAN NIGHTS

CHILDREN'S COLLECTION

Dados Internacionais de Catalogação na Publicação (CIP) de acordo com ISBD

J76f	Jones, Kellie
	The fisherman and the genie / adaptado por Kellie Jones. – Jandira : W. Books, 2025.
	128 p. ; 12,8cm x 19,8cm. – (The Arabian nights)

ISBN: 978-65-5294-174-9

1. Literatura infantojuvenil. 2. Contos. 3. Contos de Fadas. 4. Literatura Infantil. 5. Clássicos. 6. Mágica. 7. Histórias. I. Título. II. Série.

2025-603

CDD 028.5
CDU 82-93

Elaborado por Vagner Rodolfo da Silva - CRB-8/9410
Índice para catálogo sistemático:
1. Literatura infantojuvenil 028.5
2. Literatura infantojuvenil 82-93

The Fisherman and the Genie

W. Books

Long ago, in the ancient lands of Arabia, there lived a brave woman called Scheherazade. When the country's sultan went mad, Scheherazade used her cleverness and creativity to save many lives – including her own. She did this over a thousand and one nights, by telling the sultan stories of adventure, danger and enchantment.

These are just some of them …

The Fisherman
A man struggling to feed his family

The Greek King
A king with an incurable disease

Douban
A clever doctor

The Grand-Vizier
The Greek king's jealous advisor

The Sultan
*The ruler who buys fish
from the fisherman*

The Sorceress
*A mysterious woman who
can walk through walls*

The Young King
*The ruler of the
Black Isles*

Achmed
A servant

Chapter 1

The Story of the Fisherman and the Genie

Once there was a fisherman. This fisherman was so old and so poor that he struggled to feed his wife and three children. He went out early every morning to go fishing, and each day he had a rule that he would not cast his net more than four times.

One morning the fisherman set out while it was still dark to meet the tide. At the seashore, he rolled up his trousers and waded out into the inky water to throw his net. As he was drawing it back in, he noticed how heavy it was.

'I have caught something!' he cried. 'Something big!'

Unfortunately, once he had finished pulling in his net, the catch turned out to be the remains of a dead donkey and not a fish at all. He was very disappointed.

The fisherman mended his net, which the donkey had broken, then threw it a second time.

Again, he felt a great weight when he drew it back in.

'It is even heavier than last time!' he cried. 'The net must be full of fish!'

Alas, the net was not full of fish. It was full of rubbish.

The fisherman was more than just disappointed now. He was annoyed.

'Fortune does not know me,' he muttered. 'Or if it does, it enjoys  laughing at me too much to help. Me, a poor fisherman who can hardly support his family, though I work hard every day to do so.'

In this mood the fisherman cast his net a third time, and in an even worse one he pulled it back. It was full of stones, shells and mud.

In despair and exhaustion, for he had now hauled in three heavy nets for nothing, he cleared his net and cast it for a fourth and final time.

'This is my last chance,' he sighed. 'If I do not catch something this time, my family and I will go hungry again.'

With more effort and less hope than ever, he drew in his final catch. Despite the heaviness of the net, however, he found only a single yellow pot inside it. The pot was small and had markings around the opening. The old fisherman was excited.

'This pot must be full of gold to weigh so much,' he told himself. 'Why else would it be sealed shut and stamped with the owner's mark?'

The fisherman waded back to shore with his net and the pot. He took his knife to the seal around the top and opened it. The pot did not rattle as he did this. Nor did anything fall out when he turned it upside down. It was empty like his belly; worthless like that morning's work.

Feeling like he might cry from the wasted efforts of the day, the fisherman slumped onto the sand. The pot sat abandoned beside him, when smoke started pouring from the top.

The fisherman coughed. 'What is this?' he cried, leaping up and stepping back.

The smoke billowed into clouds. The clouds stretched out like the thick fog across the shore and water. When all the smoke had left the pot, it gathered back

together to make one mass. The mass became a monster.

The fisherman fell onto the sand again, trembling with fright too hard to run away. He could only stare up, up, up at the genie, and wait for what he was sure would be his death.

Sure enough, a booming voice said: 'Have you any last words before I kill you?'

The fisherman was knocked back onto his elbows by the sound.

'W-w-why kill me?' he stammered. 'I have set you free!'

'That is true,' said the genie. 'Very well, then I will grant you one favour, and that is to choose *how* I kill you.'

'But why must you kill me at all?' protested the fisherman. 'What have I done to you?'

'Nothing,' said the genie. 'But long ago, I led a rebellion against the King of the Genies, King Solomon. To punish me, he locked me away in that pot. He secured it with his seal and cast a spell to prevent my escape. Then he threw the pot into the sea where I have been ever since.

'At first, I vowed that if anyone were to find and free me within one hundred years of my captivity,

rebellion
An armed fight or fighting against a government or leader.

captivity
When someone is held prisoner.

then I would make that person rich. That did not happen, so I vowed that if anyone were to find and free me within *two* hundred years, then I would give that person all the treasures in the world. That did not happen either. It was the same for three hundred years, when I vowed to give my rescuer three wishes. No one came.

'After that, I grew angry. Rather than rewarding my rescuer, I vowed to punish them for taking so long. The only gift I would grant them would be to choose

how they died – and here we are,'
concluded the genie. *'Now choose.'*

The fisherman thought this was
very unfair. 'What an unlucky
man I am to have freed you! I beg
you, spare my life.'

'Impossible,' said the genie.
'Stop wasting time.'

He was right, the fisherman was wasting time – or rather he was using it to hatch a plan.

'Since I must die,' the fisherman said, 'and before I choose how, tell me, were you *truly* inside that pot?'

'Yes, I was.'

'But look how big you are,' said the fisherman. 'That pot could not hold even one of your feet. How can I believe you?'

'Believe your own eyes,' said the genie, and he began to change himself back into smoke. The smoke spread out across the

sand and sea as it had before.
Then it collected itself back
together and poured into the pot.
'Do you believe it now, fisherman?'
came an echoing voice, once all the
smoke had funnelled away.

The fisherman did not answer.
In a flash he seized the enchanted
lid and fitted it back onto the pot.

'Now, genie,' he cried, 'shall I let
you choose the manner
of *your* death? Or
shall I simply throw
you back into the sea
where I found you?
I promise I will see to it that no

other fisherman casts his net there. I would not want anyone else to haul you up again only to be threatened for his trouble.'

The genie railed against his old prison, but he could not escape because of the magic in Solomon's seal. So he tried to escape through cunning.

'If you will let me out,' he said. 'I promise to repay you for your trouble instead of punishing you.'

'No,' said the fisherman. 'For I believe you will treat me as the Greek king treated the doctor Douban.'

'And how was that?' the genie wondered.

So the fisherman told him …

Chapter 2

The Story of the Greek King and Doctor Douban

In the country of Zouman, in Persia, there lived a Greek king. This king had a disease known as leprosy, which none of his doctors could cure. For now, the king could still move normally, but he

Persia

An ancient empire in southwestern Asia, now called Iran.

leprosy

A skin and nerve disease that causes sores and loss of feeling in the body.

had begun wearing a bandage around his left hand because it was covered in sores. He had also been told that the disease would eventually kill him, and he was very afraid of dying.

Then one day a new doctor came to his court. His name was Douban. He was very clever, with knowledge of several languages and of herbs and medicine from around the world.

'Sire,' said Douban to the Greek king. 'If you will follow my instructions, I promise to cure your illness.'

'If you are clever enough to do that,' said the king, 'I promise to make you and your family rich forever.'

Douban went back to his house and hollowed out the wooden handle of a polo club, which he filled with herbs he had discovered on his travels. Afterwards he made a ball, and the next day he took both objects to the king.

'Here, Your Majesty. This is your cure,' he said.

'This?' said the king. 'This is just a club for playing polo.'

'This club is full of medicine.
You will begin to smell the herbs
and feel a warm glow through your
body as you play the game. Then
you must take a long hot bath
before sleeping. In the morning
you will be cured.'

The king looked doubtful, but he was also desperate. He took the club and the ball, and played a lively game of polo. The more he turned his horse and swung the club, the more he felt the "glow" the doctor had spoken of. The medicine was absorbed through the warm skin of his hand. Soon the smell grew so strong that he was eager to return to the palace and take a bath. Afterwards he fell fast asleep. In the morning, he was cured.

'I do not believe it!' he cried joyfully. 'Bring me the doctor Douban immediately.'

The king kept his word, showing the doctor every sign of gratitude for his service and showering him with riches. From the shadows, the eyes of the king's grand-vizier watched jealously. Until then, *he* had been the king's favourite, and this turn of events made him determined to ruin the doctor Douban.

'Your Majesty,' he said one day, after asking to speak with the king

grand-vizier

Someone like a modern-day prime minister. They did not just advise royal families in the old Turkish empire and in Islamic countries, they represented them and led the government. More powerful than a vizier.

privately about an important matter. 'I am deeply concerned.'

'About what?' asked the king.

'About your new doctor. I worry that you are putting too much trust in a man whose loyalty has not been proved. How do you know that he is not a spy and part of some plot to kill you?'

'Kill me? He saved my life!
I will not hear a bad word against
him. You are only jealous and
seek to turn me against him.
You will not succeed. I remember
too well the father's regret over
the parrot.'

'What father, Sire?' asked the grand-vizier. 'What parrot?'

'It is a story about not believing everything you hear before considering why someone might be saying it ...'

Chapter 3

The Story of the Father and the Parrot

There once was a father who had a headstrong young daughter he loved very much. His wife, the girl's mother, had passed away quite recently, and since then the father had tried to stay home with his daughter as much as possible. But one day he had to leave for work.

Before he left, the father went to the market to buy a gift for his daughter. The gift was a very expensive blue-and-yellow parrot from a stall selling many other exotic birds and animals. The man chose the parrot because it could talk almost as well as a person.

He hoped that it would keep his daughter company while he was gone.

As the man carried the bird home with him in its cage, it said things about the market that made him laugh.

'Do not trust the spice merchant!' it squawked. And, 'The best fruit is at the back!'

When the father gave the parrot to his daughter, she was delighted. 'He is beautiful!' she cried, stroking the feathered breast with a gentle finger.

merchant
Someone who buys and sells goods.

'Not real silk!' squawked the parrot. 'Ramie!'

The girl and her father laughed, and their parting was not as sad as it might have been without the parrot to lighten the mood.

'Take good care of your new friend,' her father said as he left the next morning. 'And be a good girl. No going inside your mother's room.'

He was still very protective of his late wife's belongings. He kept her room just as it had been on

---

ramie
A fabric made from a nettle plant.
It is sometimes mistaken for silk or
linen, which are more expensive.

the day she died. Not even the servants were allowed inside it to clean.

The father left and the girl did as she had been told, taking care of the parrot and staying out of her mother's room. The bird made her feel less lonely, but one day she woke from a nightmare and missed the comfort of her mother terribly.

At first, she hovered by the bedroom door with the parrot on her shoulder. He was squawking gossip about

the servants. Things such as:
'Broken! You broke it!' And:
'Sitting in the master's chair!'

After some time, the girl
went inside her mother's room.
She did not fix the cushions on
the bed, or trail her hands over
the netting that hung from it
as she had used to. She did not
want to leave any sign that she
had been there.

She was almost ready to
leave when a glint of light from
her mother's table drew her
to it. It was a glass bottle of
amber-coloured perfume. The

girl opened the little bottle and inhaled her mother's scent. Then she put it back in the exact same place and left, making sure that none of the servants saw her.

Her father returned the next day. He hugged his daughter and asked if she had been good while he was gone.

'Yes, father,' she replied. But the bird on her shoulder squawked: 'Mother's room!'

'What is this?' her father said. 'Did you go inside your mother's room?'

'No, father,' the girl lied.

'Yes, father!' said the parrot.

'Ignore him,' said the girl. 'He talks nonsense.'

To see who was telling the truth, the father went into his late wife's room and looked for anything that might have been moved. The moment he opened the door, he caught the scent of perfume.

He scolded his daughter for disobeying him, and his return was not as happy as it might have been without the parrot telling tales. The girl grew angry at the bird, who was meant to be her friend. That night, she put the parrot in its cage rather than letting it fly free as usual. She covered the cage with a cloth and spun it round and round, repeating the words 'Storm in the night!' with each pass.

Occasionally she stopped to take turns flashing light from a lantern ('Lightning!' she said) and banging a pot ('Thunder!' she added). Finally, she sprinkled water over the cage and fanned it from all sides ('Rain and wind!').

This went on for long enough that by morning the bird was very ruffled, and too dizzy and dazzled to know what had really happened.

'What is wrong with him?' the father asked over breakfast, when the bird seemed quieter than usual.

The daughter did not answer, but the parrot did. 'Storm in the night!' it squawked.

The father frowned. 'There was no storm in the night.'

'Wind!' insisted the parrot. 'Rain! Thunder! Lightning!'

'I told you he talks nonsense.' The daughter shrugged. 'That is why you should not trust what a bird says over me.'

All day the parrot squawked about his sleepless night, and the daughter sulked alone in her room. When she joined her father again that evening, she saw that the birdcage was empty.

'Where's my bird?' she asked.

'I took him back to the market,' her father replied. 'I did not pay good money for a bird that talks nonsense over and over again.'

The girl was shocked – she still loved her pet very much.

'But it was not nonsense!' she cried. 'For him it was as if there was a storm last night.'

When she told her father what
had happened and pleaded with
him, he went to the market to try
to buy the bird back. But it had
already been sold to a new owner.

'That,' concluded the Greek
king, 'is why I will
not listen to what
you say against the
doctor Douban.
I will keep him
by my side rather
than make the

same mistake the father made by getting rid of something rare and special because of a lie.'

'I am not lying, Your Majesty,' said the grand-vizier. 'I say this out of concern for you. Besides, is Douban rarer and more special than you are? Is his life more important than yours?'

The king frowned. No, he did not think that any doctor's life was more important than his own. Nevertheless, he insisted, 'As I do not believe that this is a matter of life or death, that hardly matters.'

'How can you be so sure, Your Majesty? We know nothing of this stranger Douban, except that he has come here through strange lands. Who knows what evil arts he has discovered on his travels?

For now, it looks like he has healed you, but you may yet suffer bad affects from his medicine. Why else would it smell so foul?'

The king was beginning to doubt his own mind. It was true that the medicine Douban had given him had smelt terrible.

The grand-vizier continued reasonably. 'Your Majesty is wise indeed to think about all the reasons why one person might say something bad  against another before trusting them. And it is true that after all my years of close, loyal service to you, I have felt jealous of Douban. But I speak now because I do not wish for my beloved king to risk himself for the sake of a doctor.'

The king hesitated. The grand-vizier had indeed served him loyally for many years, whereas he had only just met Douban. And a king owed it to his people and his court not to risk his life over a mere doctor.

'You truly believe that Douban is here to kill me?' he asked.

The grand-vizier nodded. 'I do, Sire.'

'And if you are wrong?'

'Then let me be punished as another more careless vizier once was.'

vizier
A high-ranking advisor to the royal family in the old Turkish empire and in Islamic countries.

'What vizier?' asked the Greek king. 'What punishment?'

'I will tell you the story of the vizier who was punished,' the grand-vizier said.

Chapter 4

The Story of the Vizier Who Was Punished

There once was a king whose only son enjoyed hunting. The king encouraged this hobby, but he always ordered a vizier to go with the prince and never to let him out of his sight.

One day the prince and the vizier were riding through the woods when a stag ran across their path. The prince gave chase, but the vizier was older and not quite fast enough. When the prince stopped, he was all alone in the woods. There was no stag. There was no vizier.

The vizier was busy looking for the prince. Instead he found a young boy wandering by himself. He was crying.

'What is the matter, boy?' the vizier asked.

'I have lost my mother,' wept the child.

'I have lost someone too,' said the vizier. 'Let us see if we can find them together.'

The vizier lifted the boy onto his horse and continued his journey through the woods.

The prince, meanwhile, had tried to find a path back to the vizier and got lost. Instead he found a woman wandering alone and crying.

'What is the matter, lady?' he asked her.

'I am a princess of India and I fell asleep while riding my horse and slid off. Now my horse has run away and I cannot get home.'

'I too am trying to find my way home. If you will share my horse, perhaps we might find our ways together?'

The woman accepted and rode behind the prince on his

horse. When they came across a ruined house, the woman asked the prince to stop so that she could dismount. She went inside the crumbling walls and from outside the prince heard her say: 'Good news, my darling. I have brought you something to eat!'

He also heard a young boy
reply: 'Good news, Mother!
I have brought *you* something
to eat, too!'

Although they did not know
it, both the vizier and the
prince had made the same
mistake. The little boy the
vizier had found wandering
alone was really an ogre. The
woman who had fallen from
her horse and been rescued by
the prince was his mother, an
ogress. They looked human,
but they were inhumanly
strong, and when they smiled

they revealed teeth like a wolf's. They used their innocent appearance to trick

travellers and their sharp teeth to eat them.

Before the prince could climb back on his horse and escape, the ogress came outside. She seized the prince, dragged him into her house and threw him into a different cell to the vizier, where they could not see or hear each other. Although the outside of the house made it look as if it might fall down the next time the wind blew, the cells inside it were thick and strong.

'Which one shall we eat first?' the ogress asked her son.

The smaller ogre pointed at the prince. 'This one is younger. He will be the juiciest.'

The mother nodded in agreement and together they advanced on the prince, licking their lips.

'Wait!' he yelped, realising that he was not the only prisoner on the menu. 'I may be younger, but is aged meat not more flavourful?'

The ogres left the prince and went to the vizier's cell, because yes – aged meat *was* more flavourful than young meat. They told the vizier this and together they advanced on him, licking their lips.

'Wait!' said the vizier, realising that they had caught someone else since catching him. 'I may be older, but I am also lean. Is young meat not more tender?'

The ogres left the vizier and went back to the prince's cell, because yes – young meat *was* more tender than aged meat.

'But lean meat is better,' insisted the prince when they told him so. 'It is chewier: the longer you spend chewing the more you can enjoy the taste.'

'And the longer it will take to satisfy your hunger,' was the

vizier's response
when he heard.

This continued
for some time,
with each man
arguing that the
ogres should eat the other,
unknown man first. At last, the
ogres grew so tired of walking
back and forth between two cells
that they threw the two men
into the same one.

'You!' gasped the prince when
he saw the vizier's face. 'You are
the one who has been telling
them to eat me?'

'I did not know it was you, my prince!'

'A prince?' echoed the ogress. 'Then you must know a lot about good food ...'

'Indeed I do,' said the prince, proudly. 'I have never eaten bad food in my life.'

'That settles it then.'

The ogres nodded to each other, and the vizier closed his eyes, expecting to die at any moment. His eyes flew open again when he heard the prince scream.

'Have you ever eaten royalty before?' the ogress asked her son.

She had the prince over her shoulder as she carried him to the kitchen.

'No,' replied the younger ogre. 'Are they tasty?'

'Delicious!' she replied. 'There is no better seasoning than a lifetime of good food and comfort.'

'Wait!' the vizier called after them. 'Take me instead!'

But it was too late. He had been so successful in convincing the ogres that he was old and chewy that they did not even want him for dessert. They left the cell door wide open and the vizier fled in terror.

The day's sun had almost set when he finally reached the palace. He did not live to see the dawn. As punishment for not watching over his son properly, the king had the vizier beheaded.

The prince was never seen again.

The grand-vizier turned to the Greek king and warned him: 'Sire, I fear you will regret trusting the doctor Douban, just as that other less wise king regretted trusting the other vizier.'

The king, who was used to being persuaded by his grand-vizier, could not resist him now. He was too worried.

'Perhaps you are right,' he said. 'Perhaps he did come to take my life. No one has ever seen the kind of medicine he uses.'

'Medicine, Your Majesty? Or *poison*?'

The king's worry changed to fear. 'What can I do?'

'Sire, for your own safety, I recommend sending for Douban at once and cutting off his head when he gets here.'

'Yes,' the king agreed. 'I do believe you are right.'

The king sent for the doctor. The moment Douban arrived, he was forced onto his knees and his hands were tied behind his back.

The king explained. 'Doctor Douban, I have called for you

because I believe that you are a spy and an assassin. Before you can kill me, however, I intend to kill you.' He signalled to a man with an axe to cut off the doctor's head.

Douban pleaded. 'Spare me, Your Majesty! I am no spy.'

'I cannot spare you,' said the king. 'And of course you would never admit being a spy.'

The doctor begged for his life until his voice was dry and hoarse. When it became clear

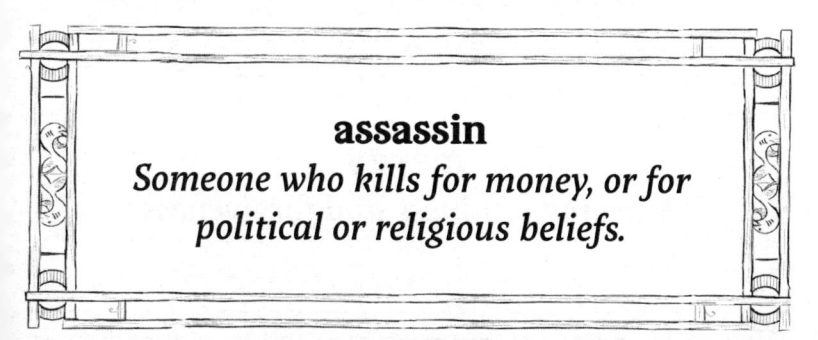

assassin
Someone who kills for money, or for political or religious beliefs.

that the king would not show mercy, he sighed.

'Very well,' said the doctor. 'Then, before I die, I want to make sure my books are taken care of. One in particular is so powerful that it should only be handled by the wisest of men. You need only turn to page number six and read the third line to understand.'

Believing himself to be the wisest of all possible men, the king ordered that the book be brought to him. When it was in his

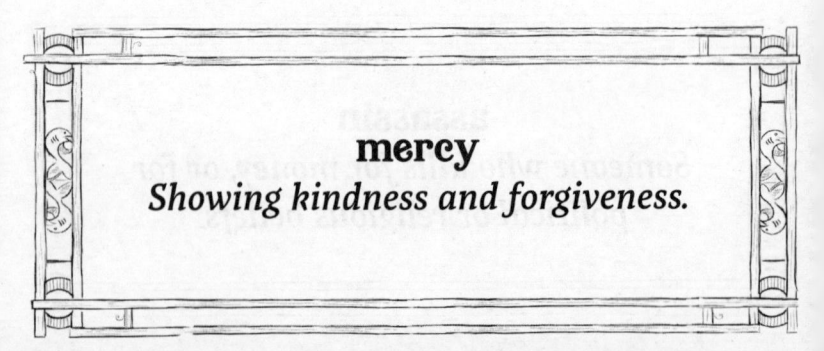

mercy
Showing kindness and forgiveness.

hands, the execution of the doctor took place. The doctor's head was cut off so neatly and quickly that it continued to speak even afterwards. It advised the king to open the book. The pages were stuck together and the king had to lick his finger to turn them. When he reached the sixth page, it was blank.

'There is nothing written here,' he said.

'Oh?' said the head of Doctor Douban. 'Forgive me, I must be mistaken. Please keep turning the pages. You will know the page I mean when you see it.'

So the king put his finger back into his mouth and continued turning pages until the poison that was on them took effect. First the king's eyesight grew dim, then he dropped the book on the floor by the doctor's head as his hands became too numb to hold it.

'Tyrant!' cried the doctor. 'Now you see how cruelty and unfairness are punished!'

With these words, both the king and his doctor died.

Back on the beach, the fisherman still held the genie's pot.

'You see?' he said. 'If the Greek king had only been grateful to the doctor for healing him, he would have lived. And if you had

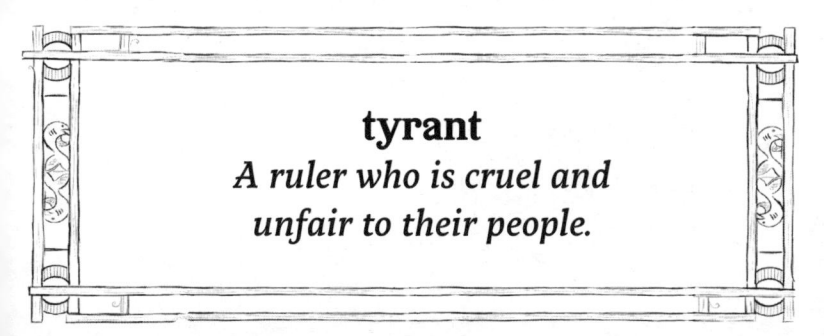

tyrant
A ruler who is cruel and unfair to their people.

only been grateful to me for your freedom, you would have kept it. Instead I must cast you back where I found you.'

The fisherman drew his arms far back over his head, ready to fling the pot into the water. The genie's voice, small from inside the pot, stopped him.

'My friend, surely you would not be so cruel? Do not treat me as Imma treated Ateca.'

'How did Imma treat Ateca?'

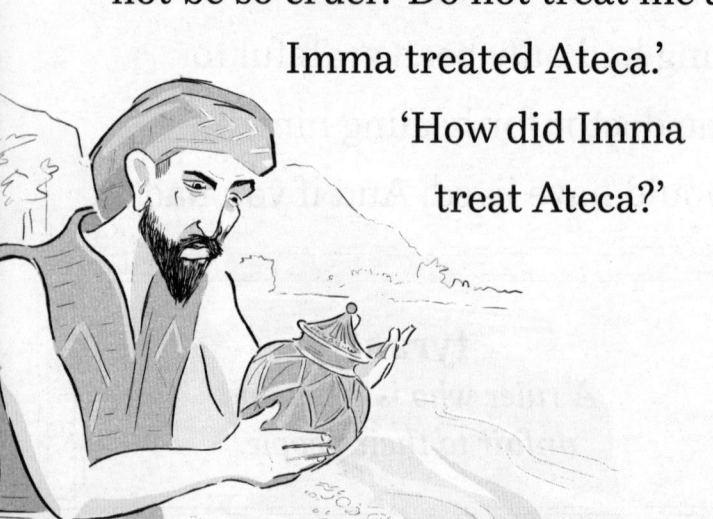

'Let me out of this pot and I will tell you.'

'Hah!' said the fisherman. 'I will not fall for that trick.'

'It is no trick,' said the genie. 'But if you will not let me out for a story, what will you do it for?'

'Fish,' said the fisherman. 'My family are hungry.'

'Is that all?' said the genie.

'And your promise that you will not kill me.'

'Done,' said the genie. 'I know just where to find some fish ...' And he laughed in a way that made the fisherman suspicious.

Nevertheless, he opened the pot. The smoke seemed to pour out even more eagerly than before. When it had gathered itself into the huge shape of the genie, he kicked the pot far out to sea, making the fisherman jump.

'Do not worry,' he said. 'I will keep my promise not to harm you. As for your fish ...'

Chapter 5

The Story of the Fisherman and the Genie Continued

The genie crooked his fingers so that the fisherman would follow him. Rather than wading back out into the water, the genie led the fisherman far past the village, up the mountain and out onto a great plain. There they found a sparkling blue lake between four green hills.

'Cast your net here,' said the genie.

The fisherman did as he was told. He could already see flashes of fish through the clear water. They were all sorts of colours he had never seen before: some white, some red, some blue and some yellow. The fisherman quickly caught one of each colour.

'They look delicious!' he said.

The genie laughed again. 'Oh, you should not eat them …'

'Why not?'

Instead of answering, the genie advised, 'Take them to the sultan of your land. He will give you more money for them than you have ever had in your life. You can come every day to fish in this lake, but do not throw your net more than once a day.'

'Why not?' the fisherman repeated.

'These fish are under a spell.'

sultan
A type of ruler or king in Islamic countries.

'What does that mean? What will happen?'

But the genie had already stamped his foot, causing the ground to split beneath it. Then he disappeared down into the crack which quickly sealed after him.

True to the genie's instructions, the fisherman did not cast his net a second time. He took his four fish straight to the palace where the sultan looked on them with amazement.

'How are they still alive?' he asked.

The fisherman was equally confused. 'I do not know, Your Majesty. They have been out of water for hours.'

Together they watched the fish flap inside the fishing net as if they could swim through the air.

'Take these fish to my cook,'

the sultan commanded his vizier. 'If they are as tasty as they are

beautiful, I will have a feast like no other. Tell the cook to keep them alive until the last possible moment. I like my fish fresh.'

The sultan paid the fisherman four hundred dinars. The genie had been right – this was more money than the fisherman

dinar
The form of money used in ancient Arabia. Still used today in some countries.

had ever had in his life. He immediately took it home with him and used it to make his family more comfortable.

The vizier, meanwhile, had delivered the four fish to the kitchen. He said to the cook, 'The sultan has just paid four hundred dinars for these fish. He wants you to cook them.'

After admiring the unusual fish for a time, the cook heated a pan with oil. He was about to put the fish in when the wall of the kitchen opened up, and through it came a beautiful woman. She wore a fine Egyptian dress and bold jewellery: gold earrings, a necklace of white pearls and gold bracelets set with rubies.

The cook watched in frozen astonishment as the woman

walked up to the pan and tipped it over into the fire. Then she took the wriggling fish and disappeared back through the opening in the wall. The opening promptly closed again.

The cook began to cry.

'Four hundred dinars gone!' he cried. 'What can I do? The sultan will think that I ate the fish myself! And I cannot just replace them with four ordinary fish because they will not be the same colours.'

When the vizier came back to check on the food, he found the cook still crying over it. The cook told the vizier about the sorceress who could walk through walls.

sorceress
A woman who claims or is believed to have magic powers.

'Are you sure you did not burn the fish by accident?' the vizier asked, eyeing the blackened pan.

'No!' the cook insisted. 'I swear to you, *she took them.*'

The vizier did not believe him, but he took pity and went to find the fisherman.

'Fisherman,' he said, 'I need four more fish like the ones you brought to the palace earlier.'

'I cannot give them to you now,' said the fisherman, remembering what the genie had said, 'but I can bring them tomorrow.'

The sultan was persuaded to give up his fish dinner for the promise of a fish breakfast. 'The cook says that leaving the fish in the herbs overnight will make them even more delicious,' said the vizier.

That night the fisherman went back to the magic lake between the four green hills. He waited until dawn to catch four more fish of four different colours. Then he took them to the palace. The vizier paid the same four hundred dinars for the fish and gave them to the cook.

'The sultan grows impatient,' he said. 'I will stay until the fish are cooked to make sure there are no more accidents.'

The vizier watched the cook carefully. Everything seemed to be going well until the cook tried to put the still-live fish in the pan.

Then the same woman appeared through the same wall and tipped the pan into the fire in the same manner as before. The vizier was as amazed as the cook had been. Both watched with wide eyes and open mouths as the woman took the wriggling fish and left.

'I must tell the sultan,' said the vizier.

The sultan was too curious to be angry that his fish breakfast was as delayed as his fish dinner had been.

'I must see this for myself,' he said, when he had heard the vizier's report.

The fisherman was asked to deliver yet more fish, which the sultan had to wait another day and pay another four hundred dinars for. Then the cook was summoned to the throne room with all his equipment so that

the sultan could see what
happened to the fish when they
tried to cook it.

This time it was not the plain
wall of the kitchen that opened
up – it was the tiled one of the
throne room. Through it came
the woman.

'Greetings,' said the sultan. Onto
the fire went the pan. 'Why do you
take my lunch?' asked the sultan.
And back through the wall went
the woman with the wriggling fish.
'Why will you not answer me?' the
sultan shouted after her. He was
not used to being ignored.

'As this has never happened before,' concluded the sultan. 'It must be to do with the fish. There is some mystery there that I must discover.' Then he summoned the fisherman and asked, 'Where did you get those fish?'

'Your Majesty,' said the fisherman, bowing low. 'I got them from a lake between four green hills that lies beyond the mountain.'

'Do you know of this lake?' the sultan asked his vizier.

'No, Sire,' said the vizier.
'And I have hunted near that
mountain many times.'

'It is there,' insisted the
fisherman. 'Some three hours
ride from here.'

The sultan ordered the
fisherman to lead the way,
while he and the rest of his
court mounted their horses and
followed. The lake was just as
the fisherman had said, between
four hills and with water so
clear that they all drew close to
its edge to watch the colourful
fish darting in its depths.

'We will make camp here,' said the sultan. 'Fisherman, catch us something to eat.'

'Your Majesty, I cannot,' said the fisherman. 'I have already cast my net this morning. I will have to wait until dawn to do it again or something bad might happen.'

'Like what?' the sultan laughed. 'You are surrounded by my men! They will protect you.'

The fisherman could not say no to the sultan. Reluctantly, he cast his net. The second he did, it became so heavy that it pulled him into the water with it. He sank like a stone despite his thrashing, and became so tangled in his own net that he stopped being able to move at all. As it turned out, that was what saved him. Meanwhile, the sultan ordered his men to haul the net back in. It took ten of them, but finally the fisherman tumbled onto dry ground, gasping and flailing as any fish would.

'It seems you were right,' said the sultan. 'No more fishing today.' To his vizier he added: 'And I will go exploring by myself. I must get to the bottom of this mystery. You will stay in my tent and tell anyone who comes to see me while I am gone that I am too sick to see them.'

Despite the vizier's protests, the sultan set out alone. He climbed one of the four hills and crossed the great plain. Eventually he stumbled upon a palace he had never seen before. It was made of polished black marble and mirrored steel. The gate stood half-open, and when nobody answered his knock, the sultan went inside.

The sultan passed through a magnificent courtyard and called out several times, but still no one answered. He entered large halls where the carpets were made of silk, the sofas were covered with tapestries and the walls glittered with hangings of silver and gold. Then he found himself in a room with a fountain held up by golden lions. Water poured from the lions' mouths and turned to diamonds and pearls as it fell.

The palace was surrounded on three sides by magnificent gardens, lakes and woods. Birds sang in the trees – and then the sultan heard a different sound: 'Oh, how I wish that I could die,' cried a voice, 'for I am too unhappy to live!'

The owner of the voice was a handsome, richly dressed young man who was sitting on a black throne. The sultan approached and bowed to him. The young man bowed back but remained seated. The sultan frowned at this rudeness.

'Forgive me,' said the young man, 'for not standing and showing you the respect you deserve.'

'I am sure you have a good reason for not doing so,' said the sultan, despite being offended.

'I do,' said the young man, and he lifted his robe to show his legs. The sultan gasped in disbelief. From the waist down, the young man's body was a block of shiny black marble.

'What happened to you?'

breathed the sultan, unable to
tear his horrified eyes away.

'It is a sad story,' said the
young man, 'but since you
asked, I will tell it …'

Chapter 6

The Story of the Young King of the Black Isles

My father was King Mahmoud. He ruled this land, which is called the Black Isles because our four hills were once islands. Our city was where the lake now lies, and it was full of people from different places and who followed many different religions.

My father died and I became the king after him. Soon after that, I met a woman. Even sooner after that, we were married. Looking back, I cannot remember falling in love. It seemed to happen all at once. People said that she had cast a spell on me, and I laughed as if they were joking. But they were not. And then I learnt that any feelings she had for me had not been very real either.

'What a shame our mistress no longer loves our master!' I overheard one of her maids say.

Another replied: 'No, now she is in love with someone else – but I do not know who.'

I found out who much later, when, I caught my wife's favourite servant stealing. I could have punished him by cutting off his hands, but instead I only gave him fifty lashes with a buffalo hide whip. My wife was still furious.

'What have you done?' she screamed.

'He was stealing from you,' I told her. 'I caught him with one of your necklaces.'

'Achmed did not steal it! I gave it to him!'

I was amazed. That necklace had been worth a fortune! I gave it to her for her birthday. I began to wonder exactly how close she was to this servant. Then she came to me the next day even angrier.

'Achmed has a fever!' she shouted.

The servant (Achmed) had collapsed in the garden. Rather than move him, my wife had a temporary shelter built around him. When his condition did not improve, the shelter became permanent – a House of Tears, people called it, for my wife went and wept there every day. By now the rumours of her magic were more than just whispers, and she did not seem to care. But it was not magic keeping the servant alive, it was the tiny amount of food and water that she fed him every hour, like he was a baby bird.

'Why not just heal him?' I asked her. 'I know you have magic. And I know you used it to make me fall in love with you. Why not use it now?'

'My magic has limits,' she sniffed. Her eyes were red from tiredness and crying. The charcoal make-up around them had run down her cheeks. 'It cannot be used to cause life or death, or believe me you would be dead already for what you have done to Achmed.'

'If you cannot heal him then let me kill him,' I offered. 'For his own sake.'

'Never,' she swore fiercely.

'Why can you not just let the man go?'

'Because I love him!'

'Then your love is even crueller than your hatred. He lies still as a statue every day and you think it living?'

'You tell me,' she hissed. Then her words became ones I could not understand, but I knew them to be magic. A cold numbness swept up my legs. I would have collapsed to the ground had my throne not been in reach. There I sat and there I have stayed,

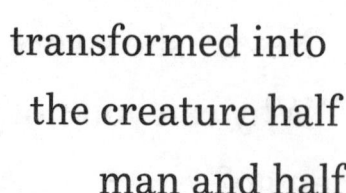

transformed into the creature half man and half marble you see before you.

Afterwards, to punish me further, my wife set about transforming the city from a busy, flourishing place into the lake and empty plain you see now. The differently coloured fish are its different people. The four hills are the four islands that give my kingdom its name. And

I only know of these changes
because my wife comes here
each day to tell me about
them. Some days she beats
me with the same buffalo hide
whip that injured her lover.

At the end of his story, the
young king burst into tears.
The sultan felt very sorry for
him.

'Where is this sorceress and
where is her precious servant?'
he demanded.

'I do not know where she stays,' answered the king. 'But I know she visits the servant every day at sunset to see if he has recovered enough to speak to her.

'Leave this to me,' said the sultan. 'I will do what I can to help you.'

The sultan went to the garden and found the House of Tears. It was a small domed building, no less beautiful than the palace. The outside shone with polished white marble. The inside glittered with thousands of mirrored pieces that were inlaid in the walls, catching and throwing the sunlight from all angles – until the sun began to set.

'There is not much time,' the sultan said, either to himself or to poor Achmed, who lay still and unblinking in the centre of the dome. He was dressed in the best clothes, surrounded by the finest furnishings, but the young king had been right – this was no life. The sultan showed the poor servant mercy and ended his suffering, then carried his body out into the garden to hide it. Afterwards, the sultan returned to the dome and lay down in the servant's place, covering himself with the fine blankets.

When the queen arrived, the sultan recognised her as the same woman who had appeared in his palace and taken the fish away before they could be cooked and killed. That must be what she meant when she said that her magic could not be used to cause death. The sultan did not know what would happen to her if she tried to break that rule, but she had clearly saved the fish from being cooked to avoid it.

Mistaking the sultan for her beloved, the queen asked the same question she asked every day: 'Are you better, my dear Achmed?'

Only today, unlike the others, Achmed/the sultan replied: 'How can I get better when the cries of your husband keep me from my rest?'

'What joy to hear you speak!' answered the queen. 'Only say that you wish me to silence him and I will do it.'

'No,' said the sultan; 'it would make me happy if you would just set him free.'

The queen would have
preferred to gag the young king
and continue his suffering, but
she did as her beloved asked.
She went into the palace and with
a few magic words, she returned
her husband's body to normal.

'Now go,' she told the king,
'before I change my mind.'

The queen went back to the
House of Tears. 'I have done as
you wished, my love. Be well
and rest.'

gag
*To stop someone speaking by putting
something over or inside their mouth.
Also the name of the thing used to
stop them speaking.*

'I cannot,' said the sultan. 'At night all the people you have changed into fish cry too.'

Without needing to be asked, the queen hurried away to the lake and said some magic words over the water. As the lake disappeared and the plain transformed, the sultan's men were astonished to find themselves suddenly in the middle of a large and beautiful town. The fish became men, women and children, and the town came back to life as the houses and shops were filled.

Once the spell had been lifted, the queen went back to the House of Tears.

'Is that better, my love?' she asked.

'Almost,' said the sultan. 'Only come closer.'

The queen moved beside her servant's bed.

'Closer.'

The queen leant over.

'Much better!' cried the sultan as he sprang up with his sword.

When the queen was dead, the sultan went to find the young king. His wobbly legs had not taken him far.

'Rejoice,' said the sultan, 'your enemy is dead.'

The young king thanked him again and again.

'And now,' said the sultan, 'I must go back to my capital.'

'Where is that?' asked the young king.

'Only a few hours ride from the lake.'

'That was before the spell was broken. The hills have returned to the original isles. I think you will find it is much further now, but I will gladly travel with you. I have been trapped here for so long that all I want to do now is go elsewhere.'

The young king saw to it that his wife was buried beside the man she loved, inside the House of Tears which was sealed up for ever. Then he put his grand-vizier in charge of his kingdom and left with the sultan. Rather than hours the journey home took weeks, and the two men grew close. By the time they reached the capital, the sultan had decided to adopt the young king as his son and next in line for the throne.

As for the fisherman, the sultan made sure that he and his family were rich, happy and well-fed for the rest of their days.